BARRACK THREE

ELYSE HOFFMAN

ISBN 978-1-952742-02-6 (ebook)

Project 613 Publishing
Project613Publishing.com

PROJECT613

CONTENTS

Barrack Three   1

Afterword   77

Dedicated to my mother and father for their enduring support
To my grandfather whose stories I never heard
To all of the heroes who fought the Nazi Regime
And to God, Who makes all stories

BARRACK THREE

"Here we are."

"Jesus...I can see how a kid would get killed here."

Vilém Rehor nodded as he pulled in front of a rusted gate that defended a dilapidated manor. He stopped the car and glanced at his girlfriend.

"Got the dog?" he queried. Jana Sladký nodded, holding up a small stuffed animal, a toy that had been a gift to her great-aunt from the son of a monster. She looked down into its black eyes. A small part of her, the part that still heard Ms. Doubek's screeches about historical artifacts ringing in her ears, didn't like the idea of abandoning something so old, so meaningful. But Iveta Sladký had made her wishes clear via Vilém, and Jana would destroy a thousand precious pieces of history if it meant making her happy.

She was so caught up in her thoughts that she didn't see or hear her boyfriend get out of the car. He ran to the passenger side and threw her door open.

"M'lady," Vilém said, bowing and offering her a hand.

"I'm gonna smack you," Jana warned, but she nonetheless took his hand and let him pull her out of the car. She pecked his cheek and stepped into the road, framing the old manor with her fingers.

"Finally here!" she sighed. "Can't believe it took so long for you to get a week off."

"Doubek's been after my head ever since I ruined Klaus' poster. I'm just grateful I still have a job."

"Me too...I mean, I kinda wish I could see you more during the day...awake...not drooling on your pillow...but I'm afraid there may be more ghosts at the Camp."

She laughed and shook her head. "I sound fuckin' insane."

"The world's fuckin' insane, babe. Even without the...y'know...ghosts."

"You haven't seen any more ghosts at the Camp, have you?"

"Not yet, but it's only a matter of time...anyway, let's get this over with. We've gotta get going so you can meet my folks!"

Jana smiled. "Y'know, I've never met anyone who's *this* eager to introduce his girlfriend to his mom."

"My mom's the best, and my dad too. And you're the best. So what's not to look forward to?"

Jana giggled, but before she could say a word, Vilém suddenly grabbed her arm and pulled her out of the road, slamming her against the outer gate of the manor. A car zoomed past, barely missing the couple.

"Jackass!" Vilém shouted, waving a pointed index finger at the car as it sped away. "Didn't even stop!"

"I can *definitely* see why Klaus got killed out here..."

sighed Jana. She made sure the dog was all right, then followed her boyfriend towards the gate, hugging the wall all the while lest another car suddenly come around the bend and flatten her.

Reinhard Heydrich, the Butcher of Prague and the Architect of the Holocaust, had once called this manor his home. A property that had once been fit for an Aryan hero was abandoned and neglected: the plaster on the outer walls had crumbled away, revealing the bricks beneath. The gate was rusted. When Vilém peered past the bars and looked onto the property, he could see litter and debris marring what must have once been a pristine environment.

Two stone statues guarded the gate, chipped and fractured: on the left was a wild boar, on the right a bear. Vilém stared at the bear's ancient, weathered face for a moment, remembering Klaus' little white teddy bear. He reached out and touched the bear, shutting his eyes.

"He's not here, right?" Jana asked, squeezing the stuffed animal. "Heydrich?"

"The innocent kid Heydrich or the mass murderer Heydrich?"

"Either," muttered Jana, biting her thumbnail nervously. She hated the idea that poor, sweet little Klaus Heydrich, who had tried so hard to save her great-aunt, could still be here, stewing over a crime that wasn't his fault. The only worse scenario would be his wicked father lingering on earth. So far, the ghosts Vilém had encountered hardly seemed able to affect the living, but if Raya could carve her name onto a wall, Jana didn't want to think about what the Butcher of Prague's ghost could do.

"I don't sense anything...and so far, every spirit I've encountered tends to stick close to the place where they died. I think I felt Heydrich Senior somewhere near the spot where the assassination happened, but I'm not eager to talk to him. Klaus, though...I think Klaus moved on."

"Good," sighed Jana. "Then...should we *not* leave the dog? He's gone and someone else may take it..."

"Iveta said to leave it no matter what. She wants someone else to pick it up and get joy out of it. She said she doesn't want it to sit in a museum for a hundred years and make people cry. Ilona has the bracelet, so...it's not like we're giving up every piece of her."

"All right...here?"

"Yeah, I think that's good..." Vilém said, watching with a bitter smile tugging at his lips as his girlfriend placed the stuffed animal beneath the stone bear. Jana stepped back and grabbed Vilém's hand. For a moment, they looked at their handiwork. There was silence except for the soft songs of the birds.

BEEP BEEP!

"Get outta the road, you weirdos!"

"We weren't in the fucking road, you asshat!" Vilém screamed as a convertible practically brushed against their heels. Jana laughed bitterly. Heydrich probably should have picked a different castle.

With Iveta's final wish fulfilled, Vilém and Jana clambered back into their car. Vilém's parents lived relatively close to the village of Panenské Břežany, where Heydrich's manor stood. They were just outside of Prague.

"So how'd you end up in my neck of the woods if your parents are from Prague?" Jana queried.

"We're not *from* Prague. We moved around a lot when I was a kid. Mom and Pa liked to change things up, see new sights and get new jobs. I lived in the village for a few years when I was little; that's how me and Erik became friends. After I turned sixteen and dropped outta school, I decided to move in with Erik since I really missed him. We only lasted a week as roommates...ha! I love him, but he's such a slob! I couldn't take it! But I stuck around for him, cheap rent, and because the town has family history. The Camp's where my grandpa was held during the war."

"Oh, Vilém..."

"He was really little, barely remembers it. And his whole family survived, even my great uncle...and he was just a baby! You know Sergeant Klammer?"

"Why wouldn't I? The sweet shop's on Klammer Street!" Jana reminded him.

"Oh, right! Well, I'm here thanks to him," Vilém explained. Sergeant Joseph Klammer was the Camp's poster boy: a young Nazi guard whose conscience hadn't allowed him to be a cog in the genocidal machine of the Third Reich. He had conspired against the Nazis, rerouting a train that had been bound for Auschwitz and saving four-hundred people.

The valiant act had cost him his life: the Nazis had hanged him as a traitor, but history and the Czech people had given him all the honor and praise he deserved. The Camp had a whole exhibit devoted to him in Barrack Three. Streets were dedicated to him, children were named after him, flowers were always left by his exhibit, and even all of this didn't seem like enough. Hundreds of people owed their lives to him. Vilém owed Joseph Klammer his very existence.

"You haven't heard from Sergeant Klammer, have you?" asked Jana. Vilém shook his head.

"I hope you never do," Jana sighed. "He deserves to be at peace after all he did."

"Yeah," Vilém agreed. He smiled at Jana. "Anyway, I got a job at the Camp and I'm a dumbass dropout, so good paying jobs are hard to come by. Pay's good at the Camp, I'm close to Erik, not far from my folks, and...well, now I've got you, so I'm pretty settled."

He let go of the wheel just long enough to tenderly touch her hair. Jana giggled, teasingly smacking his hand away.

"You're gonna make me puke," she said. "The Camp's made you sentimental."

"I guess..." sighed Vilém. "I've just learned to appreciate what I have."

"Well, I'm glad you ended up in the village, and I'm glad you got a job at the Camp. Grandma's so much happier now, and you made Iveta and Raya happy. You basically saved them from being stuck in the barracks. You're kind of a hero."

Vilém felt blood rush to his cheeks and he gripped the steering wheel tightly. He didn't want to outright deny such a statement since he knew Jana would merely continue to insist that he was a hero, but he knew he wasn't. The idea of using that word to describe himself in a world where people like Joseph Klammer existed...he shook his head. No, he wasn't a hero. He was just a janitor, trying to clean up the mess that the actual heroes and villains had left behind.

"*Vil-Vil!*"

They pulled in front of the Rehor residence and Lida Rehor ran out of the house, waving both arms. Vilém opened the car door and his mother tugged him into a tight embrace.

"Hey, Mama!" he laughed, kissing Lida's cheeks. Perhaps it was a side effect of being friends with Erik and knowing how horrible some mothers could be, but he had never been shy about being a Mama's Boy. The day he didn't kiss his mother and call her "Mama" was the day he lost his soul.

"Oh, I wish you were wearing your guard uniform!" Lida cried. "I saw that picture you posted on the Facebook! You're so handsome!"

"Mama, I wear that uniform too much," chuckled Vilém as Lida pinched his cheeks and examined him to make sure he was sufficiently fed.

"Have you...?"

"Been eating?" he snickered.

"Not just microwave dinners!" Lida said, wagging her finger in his face.

"Yes, Mama, and very well thanks to..."

"Jana!" Lida shrieked as Jana ventured from the car. Vilém laughed as his mother engulfed his girlfriend in a bone-shattering hug.

"Goodness, you're even lovelier in person!" Lida cried.

"Thank you, Mrs. Rehor," Jana choked, already overwhelmed by the Rehors' friendliess. Lida pushed Vilém and Jana into the house, drowning Jana in compliments all the while.

"Oh, cactuses!" Jana exclaimed when she entered the

Rehors' family room and saw an army of cacti standing guard: five cacti on the windowsill, a cactus on every tabletop, there were even a few small succulents perched on top of the television. An older man, Tomas Rehor, was sitting before the cactus-clad TV, watching soccer.

"Hey, old man!" Vilém said, clapping his father on the shoulder and kissing his forehead. "How's the game?"

"Horrible as ever," Tomas said, standing up, stretching, and grinning at Jana. Tomas Rehor looked good for his age; muscular and tall, with an impressive handlebar moustache perched above his thin lips.

"Vilém, for God's sake, I've told ya' to stop blackmailing pretty girls into datin' ya!" joked Tomas, shaking Jana's hand. "C'mon, she's way out of your league! You don't expect me to believe she actually *wants* to date your ugly arse, do ya?"

"Get his phone off him, I'll delete the pictures," Jana whispered. Tomas laughed and winked at his son, a silent statement of approval. He liked her already. Vilém winked back before letting his eyes wander about the room, examining the cacti.

"Hey, where's Steve?" Vilém asked.

"Oh, Vil-Vil, Steve died…" sighed Lida, and Vilém gasped as though she had just announced the demise of his childhood dog.

"Not Steve!" he cried. Jana, confused, scrutinized the cacti, realizing right then that every plant had a name painted onto its pot.

"Uhhh…should I ask about the cactuses?" Jana said. Vilém and Lida both laughed while Tomas threw up his hands.

"Oh, God, you opened Pandora's Box, Jana!" he cried. "Lida-love, explain the cactuses!"

Lida took Jana by the hand and led her to the staircase. The Rehors had carefully hung up a plethora of pictures. The youngest members hung above the bottom steps while Vilém's forefathers were displayed above the top stair.

Jana paused to admire a picture of eight-year-old Vilém making a face like a dying fish as Tomas held him in a headlock. Much to Vilém's relief, however, Lida didn't allow her to linger by her boyfriend's old pictures and stock up on blackmail material. She led Jana to the top of the staircase, pointing to a black-and-white family photograph. A woman and a man, both sporting curly black hair and wide smiles. The woman held a toddler in her arms while a grinning eleven-year-old sat on the man's shoulders.

"This is from the end of the war, when they were finally free. My grandmother, Rebecca," Lida gestured to the woman. "She ran a flower shop before the war, and my grandpa Sam—he was friends with Sergeant Joseph Klammer! He was a gardener by trade and the Nazis made him tend their grounds, but Sergeant Klammer was always kind to him."

"We were just talking on the way here," Jana said, smiling at her boyfriend. "Vilém said he was on Klammer's Train."

"Him, Rebecca, my uncle Daniel." Lida pointed to the youngest child. "And my father, Fabian."

She tapped the image of the smiling older boy with her finger and said, "Now my grandma and grandpa and Uncle Danny, all of them had green thumbs, loved plants.

But poor Dad—he loved plants, but he killed everything he touched! The only plant that could survive him were cactuses, and he loved them. I grew up with cactuses everywhere and I like to carry on the tradition now that he's gone."

"His wife, my grandma, she was allergic to pretty much everything," Vilém explained. "And since they lived with us when I was little, that meant I could never get a dog or indoor cat or...well, anything with fur. Only pet I ever had was this tabby, and he was half feral and could only live in the garage. Loved him, but it wasn't the same. Grandpa felt bad about it, so he'd let me and my sisters name the cactuses and keep them as pets. We'd paint their names on their pots, it was a lot of fun. We still name the new ones we get. It's a tradition now, a tradition to honor him."

"That's so sweet!" Jana chirped. She looked at the pictures and pointed to an image of a curly-haired man in a white lab coat. "Is this Fabian?"

"No, that's Danny! They both have the curly hair, haha!" Lida said. She gestured to a photo of a bespectacled man dressed in paint-stained overalls. He held a paint roller aloft like a knight wielding a mighty sword and grinned as he repainted the walls of a synagogue.

"This is him! Danny was the ambitious one, went the doctor route, but Dad was a quiet guy. Painted for a living, painted when he retired. Never stopped painting things."

"I've still got all the birdhouses we painted in my room," Vilém said.

"Never get rid of them," Jana commanded. "Or the cactuses. Poor Steve..."

"Steve was strong, but it was his time to go..." Lida sighed. "I say we toast in his honor. Tomas, get dinner started, I'm getting wine!"

The Rehors spoiled Jana with wine, food, and embarrassing stories to hold over Vilém's head. They stayed up stupidly late, laughing and drinking until Lida finally corked the wine and escorted Jana to Vilém's little sister's room.

"Emma won't mind if you mess with her stuff!" Vilém assured his girlfriend, pecking her cheek.

"I'll try not to anyway," Jana promised.

"Oh, please, dear, make yourself comfortable," Lida said. "You're a positively wonderful girl! Vilém is lucky to have found someone so special."

"Oh, trust me, Mrs. Rehor," Jana said, grasping her boyfriend's hand and smirking. "Vilém's the special one."

IN THE EARLY HOURS, before the sun had even considered awakening, Jana found herself possessed by an urge for a well-past-midnight snack. She slipped out of Emma's room and crept towards the staircase only to find her path impeded: Vilém was sitting on the top step, gazing up at the frozen visage of his grandfather.

"Hey, dummy, trouble sleeping?" Jana said, tapping him on the shoulder and plopping down beside him. Vilém smiled gently and shook his head.

"Nah...just hanging with my grandpa," he laughed, and she realized right away that he was upset. Without asking any probing questions, she wrapped her arms around his neck, gently hugging him, offering a silent assurance that she would listen if he wished to talk and wouldn't be offended if he didn't.

He opted to speak. "He was really great. I love all my grandparents, but he was like a big teddy bear. There when you needed him, quiet and just...there. Never helped me with my homework, didn't really give big gifts like Great-Uncle Danny, but...he kinda didn't have to. He was just super happy all the time, and he was always ready to paint stuff or listen to me blab about school."

He sighed and picked at the peeling paint on the wall. "I dunno. There's a little selfish part of me that wishes he had some unfinished business. I was an asshole teenager when he died..."

"You didn't...like...*argue* before he died, did you?" Jana asked, and Vilém shook his head.

"No, no, I was just, y'know, an asshole teenager. I just feel like I didn't...say enough, do enough to show him I loved him. I feel like now I kinda...feel more and I wanna show it. I appreciate everything he went through and I appreciate how happy he was despite it all and I appreciate the great life he gave me. I feel like I could say goodbye better than I did, but..."

He looked at his girlfriend, smiling bitterly as he said, "I know he died like he lived. He died happy, so he's...gone."

Jana kissed her boyfriend's nose and slid her hand into his, resting her head on his shoulder. "Vilém, he's looking down on you and smiling," she assured him. "I meant it when I said you were special. You see ghosts and you don't...run to make a buck, you try to help them. You're a hero. He'd be so proud of you."

Vilém smiled at her even as that word—*hero*—grated on his soul. He looked up at his grandfather's smiling face and winced. He knew he didn't have to do anything to make his grandpa proud. Fabian would have been proud of him even if he were a normal security guard at a camp without ghosts. As long as Vilém was a good and happy man, Fabian Svoboda would be smiling upon him.

But that moniker that Jana was so determined to attach to him...it didn't feel right. Appropriating that word made him feel like a thief. All he did was listen to stories. His sweet grandfather, who had lived through the Camp's torments as a mere child, deserved the title far more than he.

"You're *late*, Rehor."

"Sorry, ma'am..."

"If Ms. Sladký weren't so invested in your welfare..."

"I'd be out on my ass, ma'am. Yes, I know..." Vilém sighed, adjusting his uniform as he walked beneath the entrance gate and into the concentration camp. Ms. Doubek emerged from the swarm of historians and students, ready and raring to chew him out. Since he had nearly destroyed the Heydrich Exhibit (a crime which, thankfully, Heydrich's surviving children had chosen not to hold against him), Ms. Doubek had taken every opportunity to lay into him. Ilona defended him as often as she could, but she couldn't save him from every barb.

"I don't like employing incompetent workers. I especially don't like employing *lazy* workers," Doubek continued. She scowled and leaned forward, taking a great big whiff of his breath and snarling.

"Are you drunk? I smell alcohol!"

"Ma'am, I was in Prague," sighed Vilém.

"Partying like some hooligan college student?!"

"Ma'am, I was with my best friend and my girl-friend..." Vilém grumbled, his chest bubbling with ire. He wanted to tell her that what he did on his weekend off was none of her damn business, but he remained mum. He smirked at his own cowardice. Jana would certainly retract her "hero" label if she saw him now, nodding along as Ms. Doubek tore him to shreds.

When visitors started giving her looks and recording videos, Doubek finally dismissed him. Vilém darted into the nearest barrack, Barrack Three. Sergeant Klammer smiled at him from beyond time: a huge picture of the hero in full SS regalia stood as the centerpiece of the exhibit.

Klammer, with his blonde hair and bright blue eyes, looked like the star of a Goebbels film. He looked like the perfect Nazi, yet the exhibit boasted that he was a "Hero German." Bouquets had been laid at his feet, smooth stones had been left by Jewish admirers, and some people, lacking more expensive offerings, had framed Klammer's image with notes that expressed their gratitude. Vilém smiled when he saw the sweetest offering of them all: a little girl's drawing of her entire family, fifty people who would have never existed were it not for Klammer's heroism.

One of Vilém's coworkers, who had been watching the ordeal with Doubek through the foggy windows of the barrack, offered him a low whistle.

"Damn, the Kommandant's not showin' you any mercy," he said. Vilém looked away from Klammer's memorial, his smile wilting.

"Does she ever?" he grunted.

"Y'know if she sees you again, you'll get another lecture," his coworker said. He gestured towards one of the large placards devoted to Joseph Klammer's exploits and suggested, "Hide behind there 'till the Camp closes. Here!"

He threw his flashlight and Vilém caught it, thanked him, and took his advice, crawling behind the placard and curling into a little ball.

He hoped he would only need to wait there for a few minutes, but the local school must have been doing a field trip or something. He kept peeking under the placard, but an endless stream of feet continued to parade into the barrack. Even as the sun set, the visitors kept pouring in.

He yawned. He wasn't precisely drunk, but he was still coming down from a buzz. After driving all day to get back from Prague, he could use a nap. He would have normally never dreamed of falling asleep in the concentration camp, but perhaps encountering two ghosts and experiencing their stories had made him less squeamish about his environment. He leaned against the barrack wall. His eyes drooped, his head lulled...

Hey there...

And suddenly, he was sitting up, yelping in surprise. The Camp was completely dark, void of visitors. He sighed. He must have fallen asleep.

He pursed his lips. Asleep. Sure.

He leaned back again and shut his eyes. "Hello?" he called out.

Sorry. Didn't think I'd spook ya'. Figured at this point you'd be used to this shit.

Vilém chuckled. The spirit's voice was male this time, male and young, maybe slightly younger than him. Given the exhibit he was sitting in, Vilém could take an educated guess at the specter's identity.

"Sergeant Klammer?" he assumed, and the ghost chuckled.

Yep!

"Damn...y'know, my girlfriend and I were just talking about you the other day."

There's a coincidence. What were ya' talkin' about?

"How you saved my mom's side of the family. How you should be in Heaven right now instead of...being stuck in this shithole."

The spirit let out a bitter laugh. *Well, that's just the issue...where I should be. I don't think I'm nearly as noble as you've been led to believe.*

"You're gonna have a hard time convincing me of that, Sergeant. I wouldn't be here to have this conversation if it weren't for you. My great-grandpa was your gardener, Samuel Svoboda..."

Vilém felt the spirit's energy spike, as though he had nearly leapt out of the barrack's wall from shock. *Holy shit, that explains a lot...*

"A lot of what?"

If you're Sam's great-grandson...well, you're way more important than you know. Hm...I guess you kinda look like him. Hair's not as curly, though. And no offense, but you're not as handsome.

Vilém snorted. "I take after my pa."

Klammer laughed once more, and Vilém could feel the spirit's bitter joy. Affection seeped off the old wooden wall and filled Vilém's heart with warmth. Klammer must have truly valued Sam's friendship.

Yeah...yeah, I can see Sam in you. Well, how about it? I'll tell my story, you'll learn some of yours.

"Let's do it," Vilém volunteered, and once again he felt himself being tugged into another soul's memory. This time it wasn't sudden or dizzying. It felt like the spirit took him by the hand and gently led him into another world. He opened his eyes and suddenly he was seeing everything from the point of view of Joseph Klammer.

Well, here we are! Klammer's ghost declared. Vilém could feel the pulse of young Joseph Klammer quickening with excitement. He was standing in a somewhat bare living room. An older woman that Vilém assumed was the soon-to-be-hero's mother knelt before her teenage son, helping him adjust the swastika band on his arm.

"There, you look perfect!" Klammer's mother declared, kissing his cheek. "Now get out there and show our men some love!"

"Yes, ma'am!" Joseph said, offering her a hasty Hitler salute before rushing out the door. The streets were crowded with celebrating Germans. Swastika-shaped confetti fell from the windows, flowers were tossed at SS men, children waved little Nazi flags and licked lollipops decorated with the crooked cross. Vilém could feel enthusiasm and pride filling Joseph's chest like helium in a balloon, and experiencing such affection for swastikas, even if it was someone else's affection, made Vilém feel foul.

"Is this Germany?" Vilém asked.

Nope. Sudetenland, 1938. Small village. Everyone here loved Hitler, and so I did too. We hated the Czechs, and Jews...well, I had never seen a Jew in my life...

The young Klammer walked past a pack of little boys. The children had dressed up some sacks of flour with horsehair and a hat. One of them had drawn a giant nose on the flour-dummy's "face" and a yellow Star-of-David on its "belly." Klammer paused to watch, chuckling with amusement as the children pelted the Jew effigy with stones. Vilém could feel righteous fury stir in Joseph's heart, the same sort he felt whenever he read about the Nazis' crimes.

"Jesus..." he whispered.

I apologize if you feel a little racist right now, Vilém. I promise that's all me.

Vilém chuckled, though he felt no joy right then. "It's...weird. I've always wondered what the Nazis were thinking the whole time and...I guess I kinda know now. You really thought you were the victims."

I did. Can't speak for all my old comrades. We were all bullies, but bullies come in all different sorts. Some, like me, really believed the lies. Others...others just wanted someone they could beat up. But I, well, I'd been told my whole childhood that the Czechs took us away from our homeland, that the Jews were our misfortune, and I believed every word. So when the Munich Agreement happened and Hitler took us back, I wanted to repay him.

Joseph marched towards an old bakery, where a battalion of SS men were being treated to cakes and coffee on the house. Joseph's eyes fell upon their commander, a dashing dark-haired man with multiple medals twinkling on his chest.

Vilém felt a blush invade Joseph's cheeks as an alien-yet-familiar feeling took over. When Joseph looked upon the man and felt the same rush of admiration Vilém felt whenever he gazed upon a beautiful woman, it was, to Vilém, as uncomfortable as it was surprising.

"I didn't know you were gay," Vilém said.

Amazing what the history books will leave out! If anyone bothered to read through my journals, they would have figured out I was an absolute queer. I guess that would have ruined my nice, clean image, though. You wanna leave now? I assure you it's only going to get more uncomfortable.

"Mr. Klammer, I can put up with feeling a little gay if it means finding out my family's backstory."

Klammer's ghost cackled. *Oh, yeah, you're definitely Sam's descendant! You're spirited.*

"Thanks! I am a little...puzzled. Why would you join the Nazis if you were gay? They weren't exactly known for...*tolerance* in that regard."

I was in denial for most of my life, Vilém. I thought it was something horrible and shameful, but fixable. I thought if I acted like a perfect Aryan man, I could really become one.

"I'm guessing it didn't work?"

Not for lack of trying, though I guess hanging around a bunch of muscular men didn't help matters. Now hush! You really are just like Sam, you never stop asking questions!

"Yes, sir..." mumbled Vilém. He felt Joseph's pulse quicken with eager anxiety. Klammer stepped towards the medal-clad commander and thrust his hand into the air.

"Heil Hitler, sir!" he cried. The Nazi Commander looked up, smiling as he gave the youth a once-over with his eyes. No doubt Joseph's impeccably Aryan appearance impressed him.

"Heil Hitler, young man," he said, gesturing for Joseph to come closer. With as much grace as he could muster, Joseph marched towards him. Vilém could feel the young man desperately attempting to force the blush off his face.

"Enjoying the celebrations?" the Commander asked.

"Very much, sir!"

"You came over with a purpose, I can tell."

"I'd like to join the SS, sir!" Joseph proclaimed.

"Doesn't everyone? How old are you, young man?"

"Seventeen, sir!"

"Good. I assume there's a reason you're telling me this instead of filling out the official forms. I realize we just got here, but..."

Joseph's heart did a gymnastic feat against his chest. He must have been expecting and dreading that question.

"My mother had a degenerate youth before the Führer opened her eyes to the value of her race," Joseph explained. "While she never knowingly had relations with a Czech or any other undesirable, we do not have any records of my father's side of the family, and therefore..."

"Therefore you couldn't submit a family tree, I get it...here, let me get a look at ya.'"

The Commander stood and grabbed Joseph by the chin, and the battle Joseph had been waging against the blush on his cheeks became a humiliating defeat. He clenched his jaw and made his blue eyes as wide as he could, staring at the Commander's face. Vilém realized that Joseph was focusing a bit too much on the Commander's lips, and he felt a volcano of shame erupt in the closeted man's belly.

"Well, young man, I realize that blonde Jews exist," chuckled the Commander, releasing Joseph. "But if you're an undesirable, I'll throw myself in Dachau. Not to worry: I think I can work some magic."

An explosion of gratitude went off in Joseph's brain, and he could only barely resist the urge to yank the Commander into a hug.

The memory shifted to darkness, and Vilém sensed that Klammer was drifting.

"Mr. Klammer?" he called out.

Still here. Don't worry, I'm not leaving...I was just think-ing. You won't see it, but that man, Commander Weber...he got caught stealing gold from the Jews we "processed." The Nazis sent him to die on the Eastern Front, threw him right where the fighting was worst. It was fine for us to steal from those filthy Jews, but how dare he steal from thieves?

"The Nazis are expert hypocrites."

Ha! Don't I know that! Commander Weber worked his magic all right, and I became a good, loyal, hypocritical Nazi.

"I vow to you, Adolf Hitler, as Führer and Chancellor of the German Reich, absolute loyalty and bravery..."

Joseph stood in a single-file, oppressively constructed line of black-garbed men, offering a three-finger salute to a massive portrait of his Führer. He let his eyes flit away from Hitler's visage for but a moment, looking to the sidelines. His mother's face peeked out of a small cluster of onlookers. She was glowing with pride.

Vilém felt the ghost's energy become icy.

"You okay, Klammer?" he queried.

The other children in the village used to mock me...called me a whore's son...which I was, ha! But...I joined the Nazis and suddenly I was more than that. Not just some accident, not a piece of filth...a perfect human. She was so proud.

"I vow to you and the leaders you have set forth for me...absolute loyalty unto death." Young Klammer continued the oath, though Vilém sensed he was no longer directing it towards Hitler. His eyes shifted from his mother to the proudly grinning Commander Weber. The Commander realized he was being watched and offered the boy a wink. There was a proud gleam in his green eyes.

"So help me God!" Joseph completed the oath, and the SS man who had been swearing in the fresh recruits slammed the book he had been reading from shut.

"Welcome, all of you, to the SS! You are the Fatherland's heart and soul, the shield of the Reich against the undesirable forces within and without. Do your nation proud!"

He clapped, and the rest of the Nazis followed suit. Joseph looked at his mother and laughed when he realized her applause was the most enthusiastic. When the lines broke apart and the new SS men went to greet their families, Joseph's mother let out an excited shriek.

She ran to him, holding a potted plant under her arm. She hugged him with her one free arm, pressing his cheek against hers. He felt that her face was moist with tears.

"Mama!" he laughed. "Please calm down!"

"I'm calm! I couldn't be calmer! I'm so, so proud! My handsome boy! You're the handsomest recruit! Oh, you're going to be the best SS man! You'll get a hand-shake from the Führer for sure!"

"Hopefully, he'll get that handshake on stage and not in a field hospital," Commander Weber chuckled, clapping Joseph on the shoulder. He must have learned to control his infatuation after being under the handsome Commander's wing for so long.

"Thankfully, your battalion's getting trained for a simple job," the Commander said. "I made sure you wouldn't get sent anywhere uncomfortable. Worked my magic."

"I need to learn that magic," Joseph joked.

"You will, my boy! You learn fast in the SS. You're not going to be digging ditches, though—or, God forbid, dealing with the Russians! I made sure you got an honor-able post. You'll be helping us solve the Jewish Question."

Vilém wanted to retch, and his disgust doubled when he felt young Joseph's heart soar at the notion. The idea of murdering an entire race excited Joseph Klammer. The new SS recruit glanced at his mother, who was biting her nails.

"Oh, Christoph, are you sure about that? Dealing with those *creatures* when he's so young..."

"Mama, I'm eighteen!" sighed Joseph. His eyes shifted to his superior and he saluted. "What's my first post, Commander?"

"Your enthusiasm never wanes, Joseph, my boy! I could tell from the moment I saw you—I could tell you'd be a star if you could get a chance! Frau Klammer, there's nothing to worry about. He'll be guarding a ghetto, helping to keep the Jews tame."

"I don't think there's such a thing as a *tame* Jew,

Commander," muttered Joseph's mother, clenching her jaw, and Vilém wanted to wince at the inferno of hatred flaring in her eyes.

"Oh, madam, any animal can be made tame with sufficient force. Wolves, lions, even filthy rats. Yes, even Jews can be tamed, and it will be Joseph's job to keep them in line until we can figure out a humane way to deal with them."

"Humane!" spat Vilém, and yet he could feel that young Joseph Klammer didn't disagree with a word of this.

I told you, didn't I? Klammer's spirit mumbled. *I was a loyal Nazi. I really thought Jews were rats. Dirty animals...less than animals.*

"So what changed your mind?" Vilém asked.

See that flower? Klammer's ghost queried. Joseph's mother pushed the potted plant into her son's arms. It was a beautiful sapphire cornflower. Vilém felt Joseph's heart plummet.

"Oh, Mama, you know I'll kill it," Joseph laughed.

"It's the Reich's flower! I want you to have something to brighten your dorm and remind you of me!"

"I'll think of you every day, Mama! I don't need a flower!" laughed Joseph, cradling the plant. "All right, but I know it'll only last a week."

"Hm...well, since that's the Reich's national flower, you'd better take good care of it," Commander Weber joked. "Or else I may have to kick you out for defacing a symbol of German nationalism."

Joseph chuckled, looked down at the blue flower, and in the blink of an eye, the memory changed. Joseph was standing in what must have been his dorm room at the

SS barracks. He tarried by the windowsill, staring down at the now almost-dead cornflower.

"Shit..." Joseph mumbled, gingerly gripping a petal between his fingers, accidently tearing it from the plant as he did so. He let the dead petal fall into the dry dirt and sighed, looking past the plant and gazing at the Ghetto in the distance.

A forest of barbed wire surrounded the Ghetto, cutting it off from the rest of the town. Dark smoke from the factories spewed into the sky. Joseph grunted, and Vilém could feel disgust rear up in the young man's heart. Even from far away, the Jewish Quarter smelled vile. Vilém knew that was the Nazis' fault: bodies were rotting in the Ghetto streets, trash and feces weren't getting cleaned up. Letting the Ghetto become unlivably filthy was part of the Nazis' grand scheme to solve the Jewish Question. The more Jews that dropped dead from disease, the less money the SS would have to waste on bullets and gas.

But Joseph...well, Vilém could tell from the anger burning in Joseph's chest that he blamed the Jews for the rank odor.

Joseph turned his attention to the dorm building's idyllic property. A well-kept lawn, flagpoles bearing swastikas and SS lightning bolts, and a lovely garden right beneath Joseph's second-story bedroom.

Joseph leaned over, looking down at the garden and noticing a man kneeling by the flowerbed, tending the plants. A gardener, and evidently an unfamiliar one since Vilém felt a spark of surprise flare in Joseph's brain. The young Nazi glanced from the faraway figure to the almost dead plant. His eyes wandered to his roommate's empty bed and Vilém felt a stab of loneliness strike the Nazi's heart.

The SS was supposed to be a brotherhood, but the dorms were very competitive, everyone trying to out-Nazi each other. I think many of my "comrades" were jealous that they, with their flawless family trees, didn't carry as much favor as me, the whore's son who got lucky. I didn't have any friends, and when I saw the gardener down there...I was hoping to make one...or at least save my little flower friend.

Joseph grabbed the cornflower and bolted out of his room, down the stairs, and out the door. He approached the gardener with more nervousness than an Aryan superman should have.

When Joseph got close enough to actually see what the gardener looked like, Vilém recognized him right away. Dark curly hair, soft eyes. It was his great-grandfather. Sam Svoboda was patting manure into place. He was covered in dirt, his overalls were torn, and a brown jacket lay beside a heap of tools. He wasn't wearing the mandatory yellow star. Vilém assumed that the Nazis either didn't yet know he was a Jew, or his star was sewn onto the jacket he had dared to take off while he worked.

Vilém's great-grandfather was decently handsome, certainly no Adonis. Yet when Joseph got a good look at the gardener, a wave of wonder washed over him. Vilém loved Jana with all his heart. As far as he was concerned, she was the most gorgeous woman in the entire world. The way Joseph felt right then as he gazed at Sam was identical to how he felt whenever he saw his girlfriend: pure awe.

"U-Uhm..." Joseph stuttered. Sam looked up, and

while Joseph's cheeks must have been red as the Nazi flags fluttering nearby, the gardener's face became placid.

"H-Heil, Herr..." Sam mumbled, keeping his eyes downcast. Joseph, standing there in all of his Aryan glory, must have been a terrifying sight for the young Jew. If he were watching this situation from a different point of view, Vilém might have feared for Sam's safety.

But experiencing this moment through Joseph's eyes, he could feel the SS officer's knees wobbling, his tongue tying itself into knots, and the deep, terrible shame he felt for swooning over a man. Vilém felt Joseph's brain attack his heart with insults. Degenerate. Dirty. Undesirable.

Joseph's roiling stomach urged him to flee, to return to the house and pretend he had never seen the handsome gardener. But somehow, he ignored his impulses and summoned the strength to offer Sam his dying cornflower.

"I...don't mean to interrupt you, Herr Gardener..." he choked. "But...my little friend could use your...green thumb."

A splash of color returned to Sam's face. He hesitated for only a moment before something—either his love of plants or fear of what the Nazi would do to him if he refused—convinced him to nod. "Give it here," Sam said, and hearing the voice of his great-grandfather made a bubble of happiness form in Vilém's heart.

"He has a nice voice..." Vilém observed as Joseph sat in the dirt beside Sam and handed him the plant. Sam scrutinized it like a doctor might a critical patient.

Musical, and once he started talking, he wouldn't stop...but I didn't mind. I loved to listen to his voice. He just...glowed whenever he talked about the things he loved. His plants, his wife, his baby. It was like watching a flower bloom.

In the blink of an eye, the memory changed, though not by much. Joseph was holding the potted cornflower, which was livelier than it had ever been, glistening proudly in the sunlight. Klammer trotted to the garden, and evidently enough time had passed for Sam to regard the SS man with a bright smile.

"How's your baby?" Sam asked. Joseph sat on the raised flowerbed, setting the plant down in front of the gardener. Sam brushed his fingers against the flower's soft petals.

"He looks good!" Sam announced, his eyes dancing with pride.

"Thanks to you!" said Joseph. "How about your baby?"

"He said 'Papa'!"

"Finally!" laughed Joseph. "If he kept on refusing to say anything but 'Mama', I think you would have had grounds to disown him."

"Ha! He'll never know how frustrating he was....but...all things considered, he's doing well." Sam shoved his trowel into the dirt, his smile tapering into a worried grimace.

"Listen," Joseph murmured, and Vilém could feel fear shoot through the Nazi's body as he spoke. "If...you or your kid need anything...I know you're Czech, but you're...I...appreciate your company. I'd like to help, if you need it. I can get away with a lot. I could...well, I could work some magic."

Sam snorted, lifting the full trowel and slowly letting the dirt fall, watching as it rained down on his already-filthy shoes. "I think you'd have to be a genie to help me."

"Try me," Joseph said. Sam chewed on his bottom lip, dropped his trowel, and covered his face with his hands.

"He keeps getting sick, my boy," Sam said, his voice cracking. "And I can't get him to a doctor, I can't even get him cough drops…"

Without a second of hesitation, Joseph hopped to his feet. He darted to his room, affection practically giving him super-speed. He ran to his dresser and pulled out a small rectangular tin. Vilém couldn't read the German on it, but judging by the little illustration of cherries on the front, it was probably a tin of cough drops. Smiling victoriously, Joseph returned to the garden, kneeling before Sam and offering him the tin.

"He won't like the taste, but they'll help," Joseph said. "And I can get you more."

"Private Klammer, you may get in trouble, giving me Reich resources…" Sam whispered. Joseph grasped Sam by the hand and felt as though a bolt of electricity had struck him. Love burned in the young Nazi's chest so intensely that Vilém could tell he was barely suppressing the urge to yank Sam into a kiss. He resisted, however, and instead pressed the tin into the gardener's palm.

"Joseph, please, just call me Joseph," he insisted, folding Sam's fingers over the tin and pushing it towards the gardener's dirt-stained chest. "I value your friendship, Sam. I enjoy sitting with you, talking to you. I'd like to make sure you're secure and…well, as happy as you can be, given the circumstances."

Sam glanced down at the little tin before looking into Joseph's eyes and smiling. Joseph's heart fluttered. He must have thought Samuel Svoboda had the world's loveliest smile.

"Thank you...Joseph...."

"Joseph!"

In the blink of an eye, the memory shifted. No longer was Joseph sitting in the lovely garden with his handsome friend by his side. He was leaning against a wooden post, half asleep. He snapped to attention as Commander Weber marched up to him and gave him a light smack on the cheek.

"Wakey, wakey, Private!" the Commander cried, an affectionate smirk masking his annoyance. "We've got Jews to ship out! You need to guard the gate!"

"Yes, sir!" yawned Joseph.

"Stop staying up all night, Private!" Commander Weber ordered. "I don't care if you're reading *Das Arbeiter*! If you don't sleep, the Jews get out and run amok!"

"Sorry, sir!" Joseph said. He rubbed his eyes, adjusted his gun, and skittered to his new post. There was a small booth set up which blocked the exit to the Ghetto. Several trucks were parked outside the barriers, and Vilém shivered when he saw skulls decorating the sides of the vehicles. Two German words that even Vilém could recognize were painted right below the death's heads: "Live Animals." It seemed that the Nazis had commandeered some glue-factory trucks to transport the Jews. To the train stations? Probably, and from there, to Auschwitz, Treblinka, Chelmno.

"Move, Jews, quickly!"

A crooked line of people formed in front of the booth: elderly Jews were collecting their bags and passports, waving goodbye to their younger family members.

Vilém almost retched. They were cleaning out the Ghetto, sending the old to the death camps.

"Please remain calm!" Commander Weber screeched into a microphone. "All Jews above the age of sixty must evacuate the Ghetto for their own safety. Elderly Jews who cannot work are to be relocated to an elders' camp. Rest assured: you will be taken care of."

He locked eyes with Joseph and snickered. Vilém's disgusted reaction clashed terribly with Joseph Klammer's amusement. Joseph knew they were lying. He knew, and he thought it was hilarious.

I warned you...I was an unpleasant human being, Klammer's ghost said. *Fuck, "human being" is giving me too much credit. I was a goddamn monster.*

"No," Vilém argued. "I'm feeling everything you did...you thought you were right. You thought this was okay...justified..."

And that makes it better?

"It makes you human," Vilém said. The ghost scoffed.

Don't speak too soon. Watch...

Most of the elderly Jews seemed to trust the Commander—or perhaps they didn't, but their situation was hopeless and all they could do was force themselves to believe he was telling the truth, that they would all be okay. They stayed in line, showing their passports to the Nazis and climbing into the glue trucks, urged on by truncheon-waving SS soldiers. It was all orderly.

Until one man, older than almost anyone there, limped out of the line, clutching his cane. His family begged him to stop, but his ancient eyes were flaring and he refused to yield. He marched up to the Commander and wagged his cane in the Nazi's face.

"You're lying!" he accused, and the Commander was too surprised by the old man's gall to respond. The old man faced his people and cried out, pointing his cane at Weber. "He lies! They're all lying! You think they'll let us live? Have you heard what they've said about us? I've lived long enough to see this sort of thing happen again and again! Our gentile neighbors turn on us, butcher us! They're doing it again!"

"Papa!" The old man's daughter, keeping her distance and clinging to her children, watched his bold display with horror. "Papa, please, stop!"

"They'll kill us wherever they take us! They starve us here, they'll starve us there! They'll shoot all of us!"

"We don't have any intention of shooting you, sir," Commander Weber declared, and Vilém once again felt amusement rise up in Joseph Klammer's heart. Vilém almost choked. No, of course. The Nazis wouldn't waste bullets on dirty Jews. They would only get gas.

"Please don't trust them!" the old man begged. "They'll kill us, and then they'll kill our children and our grandchildren!"

The old man's speech started to cause a stir. A few Jews tried to sneak away, but they were brutally forced back into the queue by the Nazis. Commander Weber saw that seeds of doubt were being sewn and looked towards Joseph.

"Get rid of him," he mouthed, nudging his head to indicate the old man. Joseph nodded, and Vilém felt adrenaline shoot through Joseph's body as he approached the old Jew. It was the feeling of a hunter approaching his prey.

No, not a hunter. Vilém had once dealt with a horrid

cockroach infestation in his apartment, and the sensation that Joseph Klammer felt as he marched towards the old man was identical to the feeling Vilém had experienced when he was just about to crush one of the disgusting little creatures under his boot.

"Sir, you're hysterical. Please follow me..." Klammer grabbed the old man by the arm, trying to tug him towards a building, away from the eyes of the populace where he could be properly "dealt with." The old man, who wasn't nearly as frail as he looked, put up an admirable fight, grabbing his cane and striking at the Nazi's crotch. He missed Joseph's balls by a mere centimeter, and the anger that coursed through Joseph was blinding.

"Stupid fucking Jew!" he snarled, throwing the old man to the ground. He started smashing the helpless Jew's face in with the butt of his rifle. Vilém wanted to leave, he didn't want to feel this, to feel like he was crushing cockroaches as Joseph pummeled the old man.

"Stop, stop, please!" The old man's daughter ran at Joseph, grabbing his arm and trying to pull him off her father. The old man wasn't moving.

"Do *not* touch me, you dirty Jewess!" Joseph snarled, grasping a handful of her dark hair and throwing her down beside her father. He kicked her in the stomach. Her children started screaming and crying. He raised his gun. The thrill that went through him as he put his finger on the trigger...he felt like a God.

"JOSEPH!"

But a familiar voice brought him back down to earth. He looked up and saw Sam Svoboda. A yellow Star-of-David was sewn onto the gardener's chest.

ELYSE HOFFMAN

"Sam...?" Disbelief and horror consumed Joseph's soul. For a moment, the two men stood in the midst of the now-chaotic deportation, Joseph staring slack-jawed at his scowling crush. Even as Nazis screeched at Jews and the woman beneath the barrel of his gun screamed for her children to stay away, Joseph was deaf to everything except Samuel's labored, nervous breathing.

"Sam, what are you doing? Get back in here!"

A woman in a nearby apartment complex shoved her head out the window. Vilém recognized her as his great-grandmother right away. Rebecca looked down at her husband in horror, but Sam refused to flee. He opened his arms wide and beckoned with his fingers, daring Joseph to shoot him.

Joseph, paralyzed from the realization that he was in love with a Jew, didn't move for what felt like a full minute. Slowly, however, his blood started pumping and his heart began pounding. He looked to and fro to make sure he wasn't being watched. Once he was certain that all his comrades were distracted, he abandoned the old Jew's daughter and ran at Sam.

"No!" Rebecca shrieked, and Sam inhaled sharply as the Nazi grabbed his arm, no doubt ready for his so-called friend to betray him. Joseph dragged Sam to the gardener's apartment building. He shoved Sam into the stairwell and slammed the door behind him, waiting for a moment to make sure nobody had followed them before turning to his friend.

"You're a Jew," Klammer hissed, hiding his shock behind a scowl. Sam grunted and tugged on the collar of his jacket.

34

"I take this thing off when I work," Sam said, turning to show off his yellow star. "So you never saw this thing."

"That's illegal...you're supposed to always have it on..." Joseph growled, gripping his rifle with shaking hands. "God fucking damn it, Sam, why are you working at the SS dorms?!"

"Because you fuckers made me!" Sam snapped. "Your commander came into the Ghetto, asked for gardeners, and yanked me out of line! I go to work for you assholes for free, keep your lawn nice and pretty, and since my wife and son are here I don't think of escaping! I'm a slave, Joseph! *Your* slave!"

"You...you should have told me before..."

"Before fucking what?" cried Sam. "Before you talked to me like a human being instead of a rat? Before we became 'friends'? Ha! Well, we're not really friends, are we?"

"Because you were using me!" Joseph accused, and Vilém felt the young Nazi's brain racing in desperate circles, trying to twist this madness into something that made sense, trying to shove this round peg into his worldview's square hole. "I get it! Act all sweet and inno-cent and then convince me to..."

"To *what*, Joseph?" Sam snarled, jabbing his finger into the Nazi's chest. "*I* never asked *you* for anything! *You* kept coming to *me* for your little flower friend! *You* offered *me* help! And what would I have asked for? Medicine for my child? How nefarious! What a monster I am! Well, if you want to take everything back, then here!"

He pulled the little cough drop tin Joseph had given him out of his pocket and offered it to the Nazi. "Take it! Take it and go back to beating up old men!"

"I…" Joseph looked down at the cherry-red tin and felt bile rise in his throat. He felt ill. Ill and yet, when he looked at Sam and saw the gardener's fire, his bravery, he felt more infatuated than ever.

"You don't…get it! You can't understand!" Joseph shouted, turning away from the Jew and slamming his head against the concrete wall so hard he almost knocked himself out. There was a slight clinking noise as Sam shoved the cough drops back into his pocket.

For a few seconds, there was silence save for the muffled screams emanating from outside. Eventually, Sam spoke.

"So…am I under arrest?"

Joseph turned, glaring. Hatred and love battled in his soul as he looked at the young Jew. He hated him for his silent lies, for daring to be a Jew, for all the horrible self-hatred he was feeling again. But…

"Of course not!" Joseph submitted to the love in his heart even as Hitler's fury-filled voice echoed about his skull. He smiled ever so slightly as he accepted his internal Führer's ire. There. He was a dirty Jew lover. Worse than a Jew. An eager race-traitor.

He looked at Sam, smiling as though he had just heard the most wretched dead baby joke in creation and found it hilarious. He laughed.

"What's…wrong with you?" Sam asked as Joseph leaned against the wall, hugging his gun, laughing so hard it hurt.

"Because I'm a dirty whore's son and my only friend's a Jew, you ass!" Joseph howled. "And look at me! Look at me! It's funny, isn't it? Imagine if Hitler shook my hand and then found out I'm a dirty whore's son who gives Reich resources to Jews! Haha!"

"I...don't know if any of this is funny, Joseph..." Sam muttered even as a small smile grew on his lips.

"It's hilarious!" Joseph insisted. "Oh, you don't get it. You Jews have no sense of humor."

"What?! We have a marvelous sense of humor!"

"I've never met a Jew that's made me laugh!" Joseph giggled, sliding down to the floor and smiling up at Sam. "Well...I guess you make me laugh."

"I...didn't intend to. I'm...sorry?"

"You sound so uncertain. That 'sorry' wasn't a real sorry."

"Well, sorry! But...you were beating that old man and you almost killed that girl. I...I don't know what to think right now."

"How do you think I feel?" scoffed Joseph. "Five minutes ago all Jews were dirty rats and now..."

"Now it's different? Just like that?" Sam snapped his fingers. "God, send me to Berlin, I'll just help Hitler save some flowers and all this foolishness will end."

"I know you're joking, but...I don't know. Maybe you're just...the exception to the rule. You know, Himmler says everyone in Germany has their one good Jew. I guess you're mine."

"Well, if that old man had saved your little flower," Sam said, gesturing towards the door, "then he'd be your good Jew. Get it?"

"Oh...don't ask me to think too hard right now, Sam, my head's spinning," Joseph sighed, pressing his skull against his gun, comforted by the cool metal that soothed his feverish forehead.

"I just...I didn't even think *one* of you was good. But you're good, I know you're good, I thought you were just a Czech...a salvageable Czech, maybe even a little German...ha! I was gonna ask for your family tree because I was sure you had to be part German...you're too good to be an undesirable. But...you are, you are an undesirable and I still lo...like you. But you're not...different, are you? You're just a Jew like all the rest. And if you hadn't talked to me in the garden, I would have shot you just now."

The very thought of murdering Sam made Joseph's heart clench up. "And...maybe I've shot you before. Maybe I've shot seven Sams. Maybe they were all good Jews."

He felt ill enough to vomit, but he lifted his chin, facing the gardener as he quietly queried, "Am I a murderer, Sam?"

"I...maybe a manslaughterer. I don't think you're evil, Joseph. You're just...a dumb kid..."

"Dumb kids kill kittens, not people," Joseph argued.

"Well...we're rats, aren't we?" Sam countered sarcastically.

"I hope so..." Joseph whispered, gazing down at the swastika on his arm. "I'd rather be an exterminator than a monster. I want you to be wrong so bad, Sam, I..."

"Sam!"

But before Joseph could say another word, a pair of footsteps and a scream interrupted him. Rebecca appeared at the top of the stairwell, holding a two-year-old child in her arms. The little boy had dark curls so long they almost covered his eyes. Vilém could only assume that was his beloved Grandpa Fabian as a baby.

"Oh...he's so cute," Vilém said as he looked at the little boy. He could certainly see why Sam was so worried about his son's health: had Vilém not known that Fabian would live, he wouldn't have given the boy a month. The toddler was pale, skeletal, and when he coughed a horrid gag emerged from his throat, as though he had just tried to smoke a cigarette for the first time.

Rebecca hugged her sick son to her chest, gazing down at her husband with saucer-sized eyes. She obviously wanted to run to him, to protect him, but her little baby needed her. Both Vilém and Joseph realized that she was pregnant, just starting to show.

"Becca, it's okay," Sam assured her, motioning for her to come down and meet Joseph. "This is the German I told you about before, from the SS garden."

"Is he...?" Rebecca said hesitantly, covering her son's face with her hands. The boy let out a sneeze so loud that it was a wonder the Nazis outside didn't hear it.

"God bless you, little one," Joseph mumbled, and Vilém could feel horror rise in his chest once more.

I might have killed that kid...and you wouldn't be here.

"Who...did you kill before this happened?" Vilém queried.

Escapees, healthy adults. Sams.

"You didn't show me that, you killing anyone."

Should I? I don't think you'd like the feeling of being a murderer. Even if you're not the one killing, trust me, it's a feeling that will never go away. Besides, I...would rather not relive those moments.

"No...you're right. That...out there...with the old man and the woman...that was enough."

The people I killed were not as memorable, I hate to say. I only saw them as little dots running from the Ghetto. I didn't look into their eyes or hear their children scream. It was just like...killing little gnats.

"How many?" Vilém asked.

Seven.

"But you saved four hundred!"

Murder isn't a goddamn balancing scale, Vilém. Saving a million people wouldn't make what I did before better.

"It means you learned!" Vilém argued, and the spirit chuckled.

You really are Sam's great-grandson.

Sam looked at Joseph and offered him a smile that made Joseph's heart roil. "Don't worry," the gardener said. "He's not like the rest of them."

"The rest..." Joseph leapt to his feet. "The rest! The rest will be wondering where I am! Here!" He shoved his rifle into Sam's arms.

"Take this!" he insisted, and Sam jumped back, recoiling from the firearm as though it were a venomous snake.

"Joseph, are you insane?" Sam cried. "We're not supposed to have weapons in the Ghetto!"

"You're not supposed to take your star off either!" Joseph pointed out. "Take it! I may not always be here to protect you! And listen...no matter what, you can't allow them to take your child out of this Ghetto. Trust me."

He looked towards the coughing little boy and said, "You have no idea what they'll do to him at a camp."

"I can imagine..." murmured Sam, slowly accepting the gift of the gun.

"I won't be able to smuggle anything else like this to you," Joseph said. "So only use it when you absolutely must. And whatever you do, don't let them deport you. That old man...he was right."

Joseph saw fear shine in Sam's bright eyes and he wanted nothing more than to pull him into a hug. He resisted, however, and turned away from the Jewish man. Without another word, he opened the door...

And the memory changed. Joseph, clutching a small sack, was opening the front door of his dorm building. He ran to the garden and found Sam, now sporting his yellow star. Sam greeted him with a hug, and Joseph's heart almost exploded with joy as he buried his face into the gardener's neck.

They sat, chatted, and everything seemed wonderful. But Vilém could feel a cocktail of fear and excitement swirling in Joseph's chest.

It was thrilling, you know...breaking the law. Just hugging a Jew was against the law. To love him? To give him gifts?

Joseph handed the sack to Sam. "I scavenged what I could, but the Commander's getting particular about supplies. He's apparently under investigation for some-thing-or-other. But there's chocolate! Your boy should appreciate that, should help the medicine go down!"

"He's better about medicine than I was at his age! I'd always spit it into the nearest potted plant. Didn't care if I died, just didn't wanna taste it."

"How's he doing?"

"He appreciates your gifts, but...I think he just needs a doctor and the Nazis took all the Jewish doctors away."

"Of course," mumbled Joseph. "We wouldn't want you rats saving each other. I'm sorry, Sam. I don't think I can smuggle a doctor into the Ghetto."

"It's okay..." chuckled Sam, reaching out and grabbing Joseph's hand, provoking an eruption in Joseph's heart. "You're doing enough."

Joseph looked down at Sam's hand and squeezed it. He allowed himself a moment of bliss, to enjoy the small sin, before he pulled away. "No..." he sighed. "No, I'm not."

The memory faded. Joseph was standing before his Commander. Weber's eyes were moist. His smile, once natural and wide, was forced.

"I'm sorry to see you go, my boy," he said. "But I don't think I can magic my way out of this one, and I'd hate for you to get wrapped up in my nonsense. You'll be a fantastic camp guard. Gerber will be pleased with your record. You'll do our nation proud...do me proud."

"Y-yes, sir..." Joseph stuttered, a host of feelings clashing in his soul. Pride—what little lingered—battled against anger and affection. He still admired the Commander even though he now knew what he was. Weber had been his friend and mentor for far too long. Joseph couldn't hate him, and the knowledge that he was betraying him...it hurt.

The Commander pulled Joseph into a hug. Joseph hesitated for a moment, but then he carefully put his hands on Weber's shoulders, an imitation of a hug. He pushed the Commander away and offered him a bitter smile.

"I'll get my things..." he muttered. He turned, glancing over his shoulder and stealing one last look at his mentor. Weber sunk into his chair and let out a long, exhausted exhale. He covered his face with his hands, and if those hands hadn't had so much blood on them, Vilém may have felt bad for the Nazi Commander.

Don't hate him too much, Vilém. If you don't hate me, you can't hate him. He was just as misled.

"He didn't change," Vilém argued.

Perhaps he would have...if he had a Sam of his own.

Joseph ran to his room, but not to pack. He found his precious sapphire cornflower. Vilém observed with confused distress as the young Nazi plucked the gorgeous flower from the pot, tearing it from its roots. Joseph ran to his drawer and pulled out a few pieces of parchment paper. He then scurried to the laundry room. Vilém watched with mild fascination as Klammer placed the precious flower between two pieces of parchment and pressed it with a hot iron.

A little trick from Sam...well, really from Rebecca, but Sam told me about it, said she was always pressing flowers.

"Ha!" laughed Vilém. "Yeah, I think my mom keeps all the family artifacts up in the attic in this old trunk. I remember going through it once. There were pages and pages of pressed flowers."

I wanted Sam to have the flower...to remember me. I figured it would be easier to press it...more permanent, and easier to smuggle into the Ghetto. And I...well...I figured I would give it to him and...confess. I figured once I left, I would never see him again. I wanted him to know how much I loved him, just in case...

Once the flower was pressed, Joseph hugged it to his chest and darted out of the dorm building, running to the garden. Sam was kneeling by the tulips, his head bowed. He had pulled a blue tulip from the dirt and was twirling it between his fingers.

"Sam, I...I have something to tell you!" Joseph said.

"Please go away..." Sam hissed, sadness lacing his

voice. Vilém bit his lip. Fabian must have been getting worse.

"He survived, though. The little boy, my grandfather, and Sam and Rebecca and my great-uncle Daniel, too. All of them survived."

I'm glad I know that now...I feared the worst. But that's all hindsight. At the time, it seemed like that child was as good as dead.

"I..." Joseph dropped the pressed flower, forgetting about his confession and approaching the gardener with concern. "Sam, are you okay? I just wanted to..."

Sam raised his head, glaring at Joseph with all the hatred a Nazi deserved, and screamed, "GO AWAY!"

And right as he screamed, something struck Vilém in the chest. At first he thought Sam's anger was so painful to Joseph that it felt like a physical punch to the gut, but then he found himself lying on the floor of Barrack Three. His chest ached, the wind was knocked out of him.

"The fuck...? Klammer?" Vilém gasped once he recovered enough to speak. He sat up. Sunlight was beginning to spill into the barrack. He looked around, inhaling sharply. He couldn't sense Klammer's powerful spirit, but there was definitely something nearby. Something different. Something evil.

Vilém rose to his feet and stumbled to the front of the Klammer exhibit, cautiously trying to figure out where the dark energy was coming from. But just as quickly as he felt it, it vanished. He pursed his lips together and looked towards the door. A part of him wanted to run right then. This was becoming far more intense than he had imagined. Listening to stories was one thing, but getting attacked...

He grabbed his still-throbbing chest and looked back at Joseph Klammer's picture. Seeing the young hero's severe continence made bravery stir in Vilém's chest. He shook his head. No. He would not run. He needed to listen, to see —he needed to help the man who had helped so many.

He went back behind the panel, shut his eyes, and touched the wall. "Klammer?" he called out.

Goddamn, are you okay?

"Felt like someone punched me in the chest. Did you see anything?"

No. We actually can't see each other, just...feel. We're not physically here anymore. There's nothing to see, I guess.

"I think I've sensed Heydrich's spirit before, in Prague."

If I can stay behind this long, he could. And I couldn't see who or...whatever hit you, but it definitely felt familiar.

"Familiar bad I assume?"

It kinda reminded me of Kommandant Gerber. I didn't know him very well, so I may be wrong...

"I think you're on point. He spooked Iveta back in Barrack Four. Maybe he's got something to hide and he's worried I'm gonna figure it out."

He doesn't exactly have a sterling reputation to uphold. Why would he care?

"Dunno. Depends on what he's hiding. Maybe he likes being remembered as an asshole pure Nazi...maybe he wasn't as perfect a Nazi as the history books say."

That still doesn't explain how he was able to hurt you. We're all dead, we shouldn't be able to do anything like that.

"Raya Pomnenka was so determined to be remembered that she ruined Barrack Five, scratched her name onto the wall. I think if Gerber's determined enough, he can do some damage too. Maybe not to walls, but to me."

Okay, this isn't safe. You need to leave.

"I thought about it, but I'm not gonna. I dunno why, maybe it's just luck, but I can see and hear you guys. I'm not just gonna leave you here to rot."

I'm not going to let anything bad happen to Sam's great-grandson, Vilém. I'm not asking you, I'm telling you to leave.

"Sorry, Sergeant. War's over: I'm not obligated to obey a German's command," Vilém declared, smiling cheekily. The spirit chuckled.

Fuck, fine. I guess there's really nothing I can do except get this story over with so you can get out. Just...please be careful. I don't think Sam would forgive me if I just watched and let you get hurt.

"No offense, but you're a little too dead to do much. I think Great-Grandpa Sam would understand."

Ha! True, I suppose. Believe me, if I could smack the Kommandant, I would. Well, no use dwelling on it right now, let's finish this as quickly as possible. Where were we?

"You were getting reassigned..."

Ah, right! Well, I ended up leaving without saying goodbye to Samuel. I was sent to this camp, to guard it. I couldn't stop thinking about Sam...but there was no way to write to him, nothing to do except...follow orders.

"Klammer!"

A new memory formed. Joseph was standing in a guard tower, gazing down at a mass of people clustered on the Selection Platform. Kommandant Gerber was clutching a camera and snapping a few pictures of one particular new prisoner, who was bound and gagged, kneeling at the Nazi's feet.

"Klammer, come down! Schwartz, you too!"

Joseph looked towards the second watchtower, watching as the other guard, a baby-faced SS officer who couldn't have been a day older than sixteen, eagerly bolted from his station and ran to the Kommandant.

"Heil Hitler!" the baby-faced Nazi, Schwartz, screeched as he shoved his arm into the air. His enthusiasm was rewarded with a scoff from the Kommandant. Joseph took his sweet time, lazily sauntering up to Gerber, not even bothering with a proper Nazi greeting and instead offering his boss a curt nod. Gerber didn't seem bothered by Klammer's lack of Nazi fervor: he greeted his soldier with a small smirk.

"See this Czech rat?" the Kommandant said. He grabbed the bound prisoner he had been photographing by his bloodstained hair and tugged his head up so both watchtower guards could get a good look at his bruised face.

"Yes, sir!" barked Schwartz.

"He's resistance?" Joseph assumed, and Kommandant Gerber nodded.

"Good guess, Klammer. He's tied to the Czech rats who murdered our *beloved* Reichsprotektor Heydrich."

"*Beloved*, of course," Klammer said, offering the Kommandant a wink.

The Kommandant was evidently friends with Heydrich, but he wouldn't stop complaining about him. Heydrich would come here with his son every once in a while, apparently some kind of father-son learn-how-to-be-a-Nazi trip.

"No..." Vilém muttered. "Klaus...err, Heydrich's son came here to visit Iveta."

Iveta, that was the last...dead person you spoke to, yes? Hm...why was he visiting her?

"Long story: she was a Jew, she and Klaus were friends."

A Jew! Her!? Wow...that's not what Little Martin said.

"Little Martin? The Kommandant's son? You knew him?"

Watch.

The Kommandant shoved the Czech's face into the dirt and pressed his jackboot down on the resistance fighter's spine. "This one was...a little *too* easy to catch, if you know what I mean. We suspect he may have gotten captured on purpose to spy on our operation and report about it to the outside world." He laughed, and Vilém had never wanted to punch a memory so hard.

"Not that the world will or should care about what we do to these Jews, but we'd rather not cause a panic. So be on the lookout: if he escapes, it will be trouble. You see him anywhere near the gate, you shoot to kill."

"Yes, sir!" Schwartz said, Nazi-saluting again and almost dropping his gun as he did so. Joseph chuckled at the younger Nazi's clumsy gusto and nodded.

"Going back to my post," Joseph said, turning on his heel and starting towards the watchtower.

But a familiar face appeared in the crowd of frightened Jews, making him stop in his tracks. Sam, sporting a black eye, stood on the Platform, the only Jew who wasn't carrying luggage. Instead of a suitcase, he held a little boy in his arms. Vilém at first thought the child was Fabian, but he realized the two-year-old was too young to be his grandfather. It was his great-uncle, Daniel, who looked to be in good health despite the circumstances.

Joseph moved so fast that Vilém almost didn't see what happened. One moment he was standing on the Selection Platform, frozen, staring at his beloved Sam, and the next he was running.

"You there, Jew!" he bellowed, grabbing Sam by the arm and pulling him into the closest empty cattle car. A few Nazis laughed as Joseph yanked Sam out of sight.

"You show him, Joseph!" Schwartz cheered. Joseph pushed Sam into a corner of the cattle car and gave the side of the car a harsh kick, so harsh that it felt like the whole train trembled. Sam cowered, shielding his baby with his battered body.

"Sam, it's me!" Joseph hissed. "It's me, Joseph!"

"Joseph...?" gasped Sam, wincing as Joseph kicked the wall once more.

"Don't talk! Pretend like I'm beating you! Scream!"

Sam let out a scream so convincing that it wouldn't have surprised Vilém if his great-grandfather had been holding it in since the Holocaust had started. Baby Daniel, startled by his father's apparent distress, started wailing.

"Where's Rebecca? Say it quickly!" Joseph demanded.

"Not here, she got away, the gun you gave me..."

"Hey, Klammer, need some help in there?" Schwartz called to his comrade from the Platform.

"N-no, I've got him! Leave me be, I'm having fun!" Joseph kicked the cattle car and Sam let out another terrible cry.

"Listen, we have no time. The baby can't be here. He's

too young, too much trouble. He'll be taken from you and killed."

Sam clutched the sobbing toddler to his chest and shook his head. "Then I'll die with him…" he whispered.

"Neither of you are dying! Give me the baby, I'll take him to my dorm and hide him. You need to go to the Kommandant and *beg* for a job. Tell him you're the best damn gardener in all of Europe. Tell him you'll do whatever he asks. Name drop me if you must, get on your knees if you must, but you *have* to work for him. I'll protect your boy, give him to me."

Joseph reached out, arms open, but Sam recoiled, his eyes pinned to the swastika on his friend's arm.

"Sam...please, I need you to trust me. You have nothing to lose. I would never hurt you or your child. Please trust me, I know I don't deserve it…"

"I trust you…" Sam kissed Daniel's forehand and handed him to the Nazi. While Sam continued to scream as though he was being beaten, Joseph took off his coat and wrapped the sobbing, confused child in the black tunic.

"Papa!" whined Daniel.

"My boy, be quiet. We're playing the quiet game now, you have to be quiet no matter what. If you win, we'll both get to see Mama again."

The boy was too young to fully understand and continued to sob, shoving his little fist into his mouth to muffle himself, a valiant and desperate effort to win the quiet game. Joseph held the coat-swathed child under his arm and, with his heart hammering like a drum at an SS parade, he emerged from the cattle car.

"Jesus, Klammer, you kicked the shit outta that one! What'd he do?" laughed Schwartz.

"Pretended he wasn't a Jew rat," Joseph said, fighting to maintain a casual tone. "My coat's covered in Jew blood, gonna go clean it. Cover for me."

"Gotcha!" Schwartz said, winking at his co-worker and making his way back towards the watchtowers. Smuggling the sobbing baby Daniel Svoboda away from the Selection Platform was relatively simple. Though the boy cried, he didn't struggle, and his sobs easily melded with those of the other children who screamed for their parents, with those of the babies who were ripped from the arms of their mothers.

Vilém had read enough of the Camp's grim placards to know what happened to the babies. Their parents would be assured that they were going to a nursery to be taken care of, and they would be brought to a far corner of the Camp. The Camp was too small to have its own gas chamber, but they did have one gassing van. All of the children Daniel's age would be tossed into the back of the van and suffocated with carbon monoxide. Their bodies would be thrown into a great Pit, burned into ashes.

Joseph rushed past the little wrought-iron gate that separated the Nazis' residences from the rest of the Camp. His barrack was situated behind the Kommandant's cozy abode. He almost made it, but here, far from the Selection and the screaming babies, Daniel's sobs were piercing.

"What are you doing?"

A child's gentle voice made Joseph freeze. He turned

to face a boy with curly golden hair that Vilém recognized as Little Martin, Iveta's former playmate.

"I...Heil Hitler, little one..." Joseph stuttered. Martin looked at the Nazi with wide eyes before glancing at the sobbing bundle in his arms. The child was wise enough to figure out what was happening right away.

"Baby?" he assumed. Joseph felt as though he was going to keel over right then. His heart was beating, beating...

"Come on, quickly, and be quiet!" Martin hissed, running to the front door of the Kommandant's house. "His little spy'll see!"

The boy gestured towards the other side of the house. Vilém was confused for a moment before he realized Martin was trying to point at Iveta's doghouse.

"Spy...?" Vilém muttered as Joseph decided he had no choice and followed Little Martin into the Lion's Den.

Little Martin didn't have any clue that Iveta was a Jew.

"The Kommandant made her keep it a secret, he said he didn't want her to give his son any liberal ideas about race."

Well, that little secret backfired terribly. Martin never trusted her. He thought she was there to spy on him.

"Why would Gerber spy on his own son?" Vilém queried. Before the spirit could answer, Martin ushered Joseph and Daniel into the nursery, his big blue eyes shifting to and fro as he did so, no doubt worried that Iveta was watching.

"This way," Martin whispered, pushing Klammer through a door inside the nursery labeled, "Emergency."

Joseph stumbled into a small infirmary. There was a bed, enough medical equipment to put a field hospital to shame, and even a doctor, an older man with a full beard dressed in black-and-white prison garb.

"Doctor Rabbi!" Little Martin yelped, slamming the door shut and blocking it with a chair. Joseph unwrapped Daniel and put him down on the bed. The Doctor, baffled, sat frozen for a moment before he hopped up and knelt before Little Martin.

"Boychik, what in God's name is wrong with you?" he whispered. Joseph faced little Daniel and patted his curly locks.

"Hush, little one, please..." he begged.

"It's okay," Martin assured him. "The guards in the barracks would'a heard him, but he won't be found here. The walls are all cushioned, it'll muffle him. The Kommandant never comes in the infirmary, I think it makes him feel weird. Besides, I always cry, so he can cry and the Kommandant won't notice. The spy's not even allowed in here."

"Boychik..." the Doctor started to say, but Martin held up a hand to silence him.

"He's doing a mitzvah, Doctor Rabbi!" the boy argued. "We *have* to help him!"

The Doctor-Rabbi offered a hollow smile, as though even he didn't fully believe in the pillars of his religion anymore but didn't want to crush the boy's heart. Joseph stole some candy from the Doctor's desk and handed little Daniel a lollipop, which successfully shut him up for a moment. With the toddler's wailing temporarily silenced, Joseph turned to the Doctor, questions buzzing in his mind.

"Doctor Rabbi?" repeated the Sergeant, and the Doctor gave him a slight smile.

"I'm both, he can never decide what to call me," the Rabbi explained, gesturing to Little Martin. The blonde boy plodded over to baby Daniel and sat beside him, gently comforting the younger child.

"What are you doing here?" Joseph asked.

"I could ask you the same thing, Sergeant! Why do you have a Jewish baby with you?"

"I'm a two!" argued little Daniel, holding up two fingers, and Martin giggled.

"I'm an eight!" he countered, holding up both hands and wiggling eight of his digits. Joseph smiled at the cute display, but then remembered how dire the situation was and let his smile die.

"It's a long story," he said. "I'm friends with his father and...it's just a long story! Point is: I can't let him die."

"I see..." sighed the Rabbi. "Well, a secret for a secret, then. The boychik here is a hemophiliac."

"Hemo...what?"

"I bleed a lot when I get a little bump," Martin answered, tapping the cushioned floor with his foot. "I could die if I get even a little cut."

"Ah," said Joseph, feigning understanding even though Vilém could feel that he was still confused.

"My grandpa had that," Vilém said. Klammer's spirit let out an affirmative grunt.

Guess that may explain why he was sick all the time, your grandpa.

"I made a deal with the Kommandant," the Doctor explained. "I keep the boy alive, he keeps my daughter alive."

"A son for a daughter," Joseph said with a nod, but Martin let out a noise like an angry kitten.

"He's *not* my father!" Martin screeched. "I hate him, he stole me! He killed my mama and he stole me!"

"Stole...?" muttered Joseph in confusion, and Vilém, recalling all of his high school history lessons about Czech children during the Second World War, interrupted the memory once more.

"Stole?"

Martin told me later on that he arrived at the Camp and the Kommandant took him from his mother. Sent her to die and then...well, I guess "adopted" wouldn't be the best word. But the Kommandant always had us guards believe Martin was his son. I still don't know why he stole him.

"We learned about this in class once," Vilém said. "The Nazis used to think that some Czechs who looked 'Aryan' enough were salvageable, that they could be trained to be German."

Ha! I thought that of Samuel before I knew he was a Jew.

"Yeah, but a lot of 'em took it a step further. If they saw a Czech kid who had blonde hair, blue eyes, looked Aryan...they grabbed him, stole him from his parents, tried to brainwash him into thinking he was German. Poor boy."

I wish I'd known that...stealing one's life is terrible enough, but to strip him of his whole identity...that's like killing his soul.

"So...Great-Uncle Danny hid with Martin and the Rabbi."

Yes, and Sam tended to the Kommandant's garden. He stayed in Barrack Three with the rest of the useful workers. Unfortunately, I wasn't assigned to guard his barrack. I rarely got to see Sam or Danny, but I sometimes managed to exchange a word...or sneak Sam some food.

The memory shifted to the dead of night. Joseph was squatting inside Barrack Three, placing a little bag of food beside a sleeping Sam.

Sam lay on a wooden bunk. His curly locks had been shaved off. He didn't look like himself anymore: thin, bald, broken. But Joseph looked down at him with just as much love as ever, wanting desperately to kiss the exhausted prisoner, but refraining. He was already breaking enough rules.

"Stay safe…" he whispered. He exited the barrack.

"Hello, Sergeant!"

He winced when he saw the Doctor-Rabbi emerge from Barrack Two, grinding his teeth when the old Jew greeted him with sardonic cheer. Private Schwartz stood nearby. Schwartz looked from the Jew to his coworker with a question in his eyes.

"Sergeant…" Schwartz mumbled. Joseph marched up to his fellow Nazi, grabbing the Rabbi's arm and roughly tugging him out of the Private's grasp.

"There you are, and with Little Martin's Jew too! I thought you went to Barrack Three!" Joseph lied. "You have to keep your eye on the Jews at all times, Schwartz. Don't let them have a private moment! Shame on you!"

"I…I'm so sorry, Sergeant! I'll do better!" the Private squeaked, and Joseph had to suppress a satisfied smirk.

"Back to your post, Schwartz! I'll escort this Jew back to the Kommandant's home!"

"Y-yes, of course! Heil Hitler!"

"Heil Hitler!" grunted Joseph, watching smugly as the younger Nazi scampered away like a frightened rabbit.

"You're lucky," the Rabbi observed. "That boy's too

enthralled with everything Nazi to question anything you do or say."

"He can't imagine why anyone would disagree with Hitler," Joseph said. He pointed at Barrack Two. "That's the barrack for working women, why is your daughter there?"

"Barrack Four is worse. Dirtier, and they clear it out too often. She may get caught in a deportation if she stays in Barrack Four, but here...she's...well, not safe, but not dead. Same as Danny's father, I suppose. Favored, pliant Jews can only expect so much privilege."

"I'm worried about Sam," sighed Joseph. "Typhus outbreaks keep happening and he looks sick..."

"Everyone here is sick, Sergeant Klammer. The prisoners, the guards, everyone except little Danny. He's fortunate. He still doesn't know..."

A terrible stench struck Joseph's nose, terrible and, to the Nazi, familiar. Vilém didn't recognize it right away, but he recalled his paternal grandmother's cremation and shivered.

"That's..." he muttered. Joseph's eyes flitted towards a far corner of the Camp. A vast pit was glowing orange, like a portal right to hell. Plumes of smoke rose from the Pit, coating the cloudy sky in gray.

"The babies...the children..." the Rabbi whispered. Joseph nodded.

"Joseph...that could be Danny," the Rabbi said. "In a week, that *will* be Samuel. What is the difference? Why save one and damn another?"

"Selfishness, Rabbi," Joseph answered, covering his nose with his sleeve in a futile attempt to keep the smell of burning bodies at bay.

"At least *you're* honest...but do you really believe in this Nazi nonsense anymore? Do you think *that* is okay?" The Rabbi pointed towards the Pit. Joseph Klammer, trembling, shook his head.

"I don't, but what am I supposed to do? Quit and leave Sam and Danny helpless? Refuse to work and get kicked out, sent to the Eastern Front to die in a pointless battle?"

"Those aren't your only two choices, Joseph."

"If you have another suggestion, I'd love to hear it!" hissed Joseph, pushing the Rabbi through the gates to the Kommandant's property. He heard Iveta in her doghouse, whimpering in her sleep.

"Fido's having nightmares again," the Rabbi observed. "Perhaps it's the Pit."

"Who cares?" snapped Joseph, sneaking the Rabbi back into the house and shoving him towards the nursery.

"Who indeed..." sighed the Rabbi, looking down at Martin's bed with a raised eyebrow. The boy was gone. He opened the door to the infirmary.

"Boychik?"

"Daniel!"

"Unca!" Daniel's sweet voice drifted up from beneath the table. Joseph and the Rabbi squatted down and saw both boys sitting together. Martin had shoved two cotton balls in his nostrils and Daniel was sporting an oversized gas mask.

"Stink, yuck!" Daniel said, waving his hand in front of the nozzle covering his nose. Joseph covered his mouth with his hand, muffling himself as he laughed, then cried.

"Yeah..." he sobbed. "Yeah, Danny, it stinks..."

I hope Danny didn't remember any of this...he was a sweet kid.

"I don't think he did, he never really talked about it. Neither did my grandpa, don't even know what he went through," Vilém sighed.

I'm sorry I can't give you those answers.

"You're giving a lot already. I'm wondering, though: what made you finally decide to step up?"

Oh, it's simple. The war started to go downhill, and the Kommandant received orders from Himmler. The Camp was to be liquidated. The Russians were getting closer and Himmler didn't want the Jews falling into the hands of the Allies. He didn't want the world to know what we had done. At a time when we should have been devoting our resources to the boys on the front, Hitler focused on his war against the Jews. We were ordered to clear out Barracks Two through Five, to ship all the Jews to Auschwitz.

"Including Sam..."

Including Sam. Of course, I couldn't let that happen, but there was no way to get Sam and Daniel out. If I wanted to save them, I had to save everyone.

"I've read about how you did it. Pretty impressive."

Whatever you read, I'm sure it gave me too much credit. I never could have done it by myself.

"So what did you do?"

Step one: free the Czech partisan and get him to help me. During my shift guarding him, I made an arrangement: I would let him go, he would return to his comrades, and they would meet me at a rendezvous point, help me steal the train. They would take the Jews, guard them, keep them safe.

The memory shifted. Sirens were screeching, dogs were barking, Joseph was standing up in the guard tower, watching as the Czech partisan ran from his work unit. The partisan made it out of the gate.

"I've got him!" Schwartz yelped from the other watchtower.

"No! Stand down, I've got him!" Joseph commanded, and nervous, eager-to-please Schwartz complied, lowering his gun and letting Joseph take the shot.

Joseph moved slowly, giving the Czech a generous head start. The Nazis on the ground, not wanting to face friendly fire, stayed behind the wire, waiting...

Joseph aimed, fired, and missed.

"Whoops..." he muttered, smirking as the resistance fighter vanished into the thicket.

Step two: the Czechs' job was to take the train off my hands, my job was to deliver it. I made sure I would be one of the guards on the Auschwitz Transport. But I wasn't going to be the only guard, and if I wanted to steal the train and change its course, I would need a distraction.

"Sam?"

No. The distraction's job would be to leap from the train, feign an escape attempt to get everyone's attention on him. It was essentially a suicide mission, but...thankfully, I knew someone who had something to die for.

"It's time..."

Joseph stood in the infirmary, gripping his rifle. The Rabbi sat with Daniel in his lap, quietly praying.

"I'll be a moment, Joseph."

"Not that I don't want to give you all the time you need, Rabbi, but I have to return Danny to his father."

"It will be better if I take him, Sergeant. We don't want to risk someone spotting him in Barrack Three and tossing him into the Pit," the Rabbi said. "I'll give him to Sam tomorrow...before I say goodbye to my daughter."

The Rabbi chewed on his thumbnail, his eyes becoming cloudy. Seeing his sacrificial lamb so worried —about his own mortality, about his daughter's fate without him, or perhaps he feared that their mission would fail and all of his people would be doomed— Joseph felt guilt strike at his soul. He placed a comforting hand on the Doctor's shoulder.

"You're saving her life, Rabbi," Joseph assured him. "You are a hero. She'll be proud of you. They'll all be proud of you."

"I'm sure..." the Rabbi whispered, raising his emerald eyes, which shimmered with pride as he gazed at the SS officer. "God be with you, Joseph."

"Just this once..." Klammer sighed. He looked down at Danny, who was fiddling with the Rabbi's striped cap, and patted the boy's cheek.

"Be good, okay?" he pleaded. "You're gonna see Papa again, but only if you win the quiet game."

"Okay!" Daniel said with radiant enthusiasm, still blissfully ignorant of all that was going on. Joseph pinched the toddler's cheek, then looked down at Little Martin, who was glaring into the button eyes of a toy cat. He held the ratty stuffed animal by its neck, squeezing its throat, futilely trying to throttle the toy and rid himself of whatever awful feelings it inspired within him.

"I'm sorry," Joseph said. "I don't want to take your doctor from you...at least he's here for your birthday."

"Doctor Rabbi's doing a mitzvah," replied Martin with a shrug. "So it's okay. Besides, it's not my birthday today. It's the day the Kommandant stole me...he just says it's my birthday."

"Oh..." Klammer whispered. "I...well...I guess it's a good thing I didn't buy you a present."

Martin giggled, looking up from his stuffed animal. "It's okay. I've been a good little Nazi, so the Kommandant probably got me something big, a big stolen toy. The other guards probably got me...socks with little swastikas on them."

"Come now, Martin: the guards here are evil, but none of them are *that* evil," joked Joseph, earning another giggle from the child. Little Martin looked at him, his eyes twinkling, and Joseph felt a pool of pride form in his chest. He had made the miserable boy smile on his not-birthday.

That kid never smiled...not really. He smiled when he was with Danny and the Rabbi, but everywhere else, when the Kommandant paraded him around and the guards gave him candy, he just had dead eyes. I hated leaving him there to be miserable, but if the Kommandant woke up and his "son" was gone, the whole operation could fail. He seemed to understand...he didn't make a fuss.

"Thanks for being nice, Sergeant Klammer," Little Martin said. "Please don't die."

"I'll try my best," snorted Joseph. He knelt down and offered the boy his hand, which Martin eagerly grabbed. The Nazi and the kidnapped Czech shook hands, and Vilém was surprised by the strength of the sick little boy's grasp.

Joseph left the infirmary, exited the Kommandant's property, and ventured back into the camp area. A terrible, familiar smell drew his attention to the electrified fence. The Kommandant was snapping a picture of a twisted, tiny body that hung from the barbed wire.

"Iveta..." whispered Vilém, barely able to recognize the burnt remains of Jana's great aunt. "Oh no, she missed the Freedom Train by a day..."

Poor kid...wish I'd known. Wish Little Martin had known, he would have fought to keep her in the house if he had...

"Klammer!" the Kommandant cried. "Where you off to?"

"I was just wishing Little Martin a happy birthday and I saw that your gardener left a mess," lied Joseph, cracking his knuckles. "I want to teach him a lesson."

"Got it!" chuckled the Kommandant. "Don't be *too* harsh, though. We don't want any trouble."

"Right. No trouble..." muttered Joseph, letting his eyes dart to Iveta's body and barely holding in the urge to gag as he slipped into Barrack Three. Most of the prisoners who normally slept in the barrack were out working, making guns and assembling trucks for the Nazis. The only Jews that remained were those too sick to move, those left to die alone.

"Sam!" Joseph whispered, kneeling beside the gardener's bunk. Sam, still terribly ill, hardly stirred.

"Sam, please get up! Listen to me: you have to leave with the others tomorrow. Even if you feel like you're going to die if you move, you *must* move. I'm going to free you and your boy, but you must get on the train tomorrow."

"Train, what train...?" mumbled Sam, sleepily sitting up on his elbow.

"You're going to be deported..."

"To where?"

63

"Doesn't matter, I *will* free you and every other Jew on the train. You need to meet up with a man named Rabbi Yosef. He will have your boy. Find him on the Platform, get your boy, and survive."

"You're going to save us all?" Sam asked, hope seemingly giving him strength. Joseph reached out, cupping Sam's gaunt face in his hands.

"Listen to me, Samuel Svoboda," Joseph said, almost nose-to-nose with the gardener, his heart throbbing painfully against his chest. "If anything happens tomorrow, I want you and everyone else to know that I'm doing this for you. Not for glory, God, not for the Jews and not because I'm good. I'm doing this for you. Because I love you."

He started to pull Sam close.

Er! Uhm!

But Klammer's spirit forced the memory to vanish into blackness before Vilém could have the extremely uncomfortable experience of knowing what kissing his great-grandfather felt like.

Er, sorry...I...well...you get the point and...uh...yeah, that's your relative...so...sorry.

"Ha! Thanks!" chuckled Vilém. "I can die happy without living through that. Uhm...did he kiss back, though?"

...Yes.

"He really loved you."

Maybe if things had been different, I could have been a homewrecker in addition to all my other bad qualities.

"Haha! You were always so nice to Rebecca and Sam's kids, though."

Whatever he may have felt for me, he loved them. I would

*have never asked him to destroy his life on my behalf. They
made him happy. It wasn't their fault I could have never done
as much.*

"You still saved his life. Speaking of which..."

*Ah. The train. Well, the operation almost went down
flawlessly.*

"Almost?" Vilém dared to ask, and a new memory
started up.

"Hey, that Jew's getting away!"

Joseph was standing on top of the train, on the
cattle car closest to the engine. His blonde hair
whipped in his face as he watched Doctor Yosef leap
from the Auschwitz Train and bolt towards the woods.
The Doctor was wise enough to run in a zigzag, but
every one of Joseph's comrades gathered on the
caboose.

*We used to get extra rations and a day off if we shot an
escapee,* Joseph's spirit explained as the Nazis eagerly
took aim at the running Jew. *I knew they couldn't resist.*

Joseph acted quickly, raising his gun and opening fire
on his comrades. He was too late, however, and one of
the SS men fired off a shot that toppled the Doctor.
Joseph heard a girl scream. The Rabbi's daughter had
seen everything.

"What the...?" Schwartz yelped, turning towards the
source of the apparent friendly fire. Joseph hesitated only
for a moment before he emptied his gun into the young
Nazi's chest. Schwartz and the other SS soldiers tumbled
off the train, and with the guards neutralized, Joseph
struggled against the wind, climbing into the engineer's
compartment.

"What happened?" the conductor cried, but Joseph

didn't dare offer him an answer. He jabbed the barrel of his gun into the Nazi's heart.

"Would you like to change the train's course, or should I?" he offered, and the conductor, evidently not eager to die for his country, squeaked and nodded pliantly.

"Where to?" the conductor asked, and Joseph commanded him to switch tracks. The conductor obeyed, and the train chugged along for a few more miles until it arrived at the rendezvous point. Joseph ordered the conductor to stop the train and he obeyed, yanking on the lever. The train screeched to a halt, and once it stopped, Joseph grabbed the conductor and tossed him out of the compartment. The Czech partisans emerged from the woods, lunging at the German conductor, kicking him fiercely before tying his wrists together.

"He'll make a good hostage!" one partisan, whom Vilém recognized as the one Klammer had let escape, yelled to the Sergeant. Joseph jumped down and shook the Czech's hand.

"I'm impressed, Klammer!" the Czech cried. "Half of us didn't think you were actually gonna manage this! The other half thought this was a trap."

"I had a good motivation..." Joseph said. His eyes flitted to the cattle cars and he watched with joyous relief as the Czechs released the baffled Jews.

"You're all free!" the Czechs announced. "The spy freed you!"

"Spy...?" chortled Joseph, and the Jews looked towards their savior, some with suspicion, some with smiles. He tried to find Sam's smile, but he didn't see the gardener. He wanted to find him, to kiss him again, to see him as a free man for the first time...but his heart was hastily reminding him of one last obligation.

"One of the Jews jumped off the train to distract the guards, a Rabbi," Joseph said, opening his arms towards the Czechs and begging, "Do you have a car to spare? Or a bike? I have to go back for him."

"You're sure?" the Czech leader said, clenching his jaw.

"He may still be alive, I *have* to."

"We have a bike, you can take it...but we're going. We can't stay here. If you go back for him and he's alive, you'll have to figure out what to do with him yourself."

"That's fine...just please keep the Jews safe."

"Jews, gentiles. They're all Czechs. We'll protect our people," the partisan assured him. Another Czech pushed a motorcycle towards Joseph, a sputtering machine that more resembled a heap of rusted scraps than a reliable means of transportation. Joseph felt his blood pressure spike at the mere sight of the barely-functioning vehicle, but he huffed, decided that beggars couldn't be choosers, and hopped on.

He sped off, daring to glance over his shoulder, desperate for one last look at Sam.

"Joseph!"

His heart fluttered. Sam had climbed on top of the Freedom Train. He stood there, hugging Daniel. Still gaunt, still sick, but he was free and he knew it. He smiled a smile so radiant it all but burned Joseph's corneas.

Sam waved to him, and though Joseph didn't dare to wave back as taking one hand off the old cycle could have very well sent it careening into a tree, he grinned so widely that Sam must have been able to see it even a mile away.

Klammer rode until he couldn't see the train anymore, following the tracks and finally coming across the bodies. He jumped off the bike and ran to the Doctor's side. Almost-dry blood stained the Rabbi's black-and-white uniform. He wasn't breathing, and when Joseph knelt down and tried to find a pulse, there was merely silence.

"I'm sorry..." he muttered, leaning down and gently shutting the Doctor's eyes. "I wish I knew a Jewish prayer, but..."

Before he could say another word to his deceased partner, a groan made him leap to his feet and pull out his gun. He aimed at the fallen Nazis and discovered that one of his former comrades was stirring.

"Schwartz..." he hissed. He chewed on his lip and Vilém could feel hesitation tugging at his heart. His fingers gingerly touched the trigger. It would be easy to put the teenager out of his misery and run back to Sam, to freedom. It would be easy and it was so, so tempting.

"Fuck me..." But something stopped him. Vilém felt guilt and self-hatred take hold of Klammer and force him to lower his gun. He shoved the weapon back into its holster and carefully approached the young Nazi. Joseph grabbed the injured teen's gun and tossed it into the bushes before slinging the boy's arm over his shoulder and carrying him towards the bike.

"You...you shot me..." groaned Schwartz as Joseph sat him on the bike, which almost crumbled beneath their shared weight.

"And now I'm saving you," Joseph huffed, as though doing so was a chore.

"Why...?"

"Why did I shoot you? Because you deserved it. Why am I saving you? Because I do too. You're a Nazi and so am I..."

"You're not a National Socialist, you're a traitor to the Führer and our people..." mumbled Schwartz, and Joseph let out a bitter laugh.

"Even half-dead you still spit propaganda! Goebbels would be proud," the Sergeant chuckled. "You're a stupid kid that's grown up in a stupid world, and I hope you live long enough to realize that."

"You're gonna get shot..." Schwartz growled.

"Oh, I doubt it," Joseph sighed. "I just unleashed a plague of Jews upon the Fatherland. They'll do far worse to me. It was worth it, though. And you...I hope you can make this worth it."

Slowly as possible, he rode back towards the Camp. The memory shifted to darkness.

I couldn't just let him die...

"You could have lived if you had," Vilém muttered. "Do you know what happened to him?"

No idea. Never saw him again after that day. He didn't even attend my execution. Oh, speaking of which, he was right. I got back to the Camp, he spilled his guts, and I was arrested. Once a proud Aryan superman, now a traitor. I didn't have a fun time...especially since the Kommandant was in a nasty mood. Turns out Little Martin snuck onto the Freedom Train. Kommandant lost his little project.

"I hope he found his family...whatever was left of it," sighed Vilém.

I hope he learned to be a Czech again. I hope he never spoke a word of German again for as long as he lived.

"And you...?"

No regrets, except...

A new memory formed. Vilém shivered. Every inch of Joseph Klammer's body was aching. He had been stripped of his SS regalia and shoved into thin, black-and-white striped garb. He had been beaten, he was starving, and it was so cold. He sat on a small mound of hay in a tiny concrete cell. No bed, no chair, only a bucket for a toilet (which, thankfully, it appeared he hadn't used yet, though perhaps that was because he'd been given nothing to eat or drink.)

There was a *clang* from somewhere nearby and the sound of footsteps echoed throughout the cell block: one set of jackboots and one set of heels.

"Visitor," a Nazi guard grunted, standing near the cell as Joseph's mother approached the bars. Joseph stood too quickly and almost fell over; his legs felt like pudding, but through pure willpower he managed to stumble towards his mother, collapsing before her, clutching the bars.

"Mama..." he sighed, finally allowing some weakness to show as he looked up at her face, hungry for the smallest smidgeon of affection.

But she scowled at her son like he was a diseased worm. Frau Klammer inhaled deeply and then spat right in Joseph's face. He yelped and recoiled, rubbing the spittle out of his eyes and seething when he heard the Nazi guard snicker.

"You're no son of mine," Frau Klammer declared.

"You're a traitor to the Führer and the nation. You are a filthy little nothing and you will die alone."

Joseph scowled, peering into his mother's eyes, trying to find a sign that she was lying, that she was only saying this because she was scared, because she was forced to, because she *had* to.

But there was nothing. The mother that had once kissed his cheek and called him her pride looked upon him with eyes of ice. She meant it. She loved Hitler more than her own son.

Vilém had always thought of his mother as one of his best friends, and had often, during his low points, been afraid of disappointing her. On those terrible occasions when he had fucked up enough to earn her ire, he had felt like a boot was being laid upon his back, crushing him like a bug. But Lida Rehor had always lifted that weight right off his shoulders. She had always assured him that she would love him no matter what.

He would need to visit Lida again after this, to give her a hug, to see the love pouring from her eyes. Feeling Joseph's soul shatter beneath his mother's boot felt almost as bad as any death he had experienced in a memory. Frau Klammer turned and marched away with a slight bounce in her step, as though she had just done something truly brave.

I wish she would have let me talk.

"I...I'm sorry, Sergeant, I don't think I could arrange a reunion," Vilém sighed as the memory shifted. Joseph was standing on a platform above a small crowd of Nazis. Neither Schwartz nor Frau Klammer were anywhere to be seen. Joseph searched the sneering onlookers, but found no familiar face to latch onto.

"Was it worth it, Klammer?" the Kommandant's arrogant voice sneered in his ear. Joseph glanced at his former boss. Gerber was leaning against a post with a noose.

"Absolutely," Klammer proclaimed, forcing his face to remain expressionless even as his eyes frantically darted here and there, trying to find a comforting thing to look at while he died.

But there was nothing. Barbed wire, watchtowers, barracks, and swastikas. The forest was distant and enshrouded in shadow, and there were no more flowers decorating the Kommandant's home.

The Kommandant reached up and tugged on the noose. "Piano wire," he said. "Traitors don't get a rope."

"I get it, it's gonna hurt," grunted Joseph. "I have many regrets, Kommandant, but I'll never regret freeing those people."

"*People!*" scoffed the Kommandant. "You *are* gone."

"I was…" sighed Joseph. With nothing else to look at, he turned his gaze towards Barrack Three, which was wonderfully, mercifully empty. He smiled even as the noose was wrapped around his neck, even as the wire sliced into his skin, even as the executioner lifted him up and he dangled by his neck, his body convulsing…

Enough!

And suddenly, it was over, and Vilém was back in Barrack Three. Klammer had kicked him out of his final memory. Grunting with ire, Vilém shut his eyes and touched the wall once more.

"Why'd you do that?" he asked.

You get the picture. I died. It lasted a while. It hurt. I don't want you to experience it, there's no need.

"I...thanks, I guess...the feeling of dying is never...pleasant..." muttered Vilém, rubbing his neck and inhaling deeply, enjoying the cool and assuring sensation of air sweeping into his lungs.

"So," Vilém said. "Thank you for showing me all that, and thanks for being honest. It's...nice to know a little more about what happened to my family. It's...different from what I was told...not that I was told much...but it's...good to know, it gives me perspective. I owe you a lot, and I want to help you however I can, Sergeant Klammer. Why are you still here? What's your unfinished business?"

Isn't it obvious?

"Is it your mom? I'm sorry, but I really don't think I can help you with that."

No! It's this! This whole exhibit! Don't you get it? It's all a lie! I'm not a hero! Doctor Yosef is! He died for his people, I only tried to save someone I loved! That doesn't make me a hero! I was selfish and stupid and I don't deserve any of this! I want the truth to get out there! I want everyone to know that I'm not a hero!

"But you *are* a hero, Sergeant!" Vilém argued.

I am not! All of these streets named for me, these memorials, they should all be taken down and redone. I want Rabbi Yosef to be honored instead of me! He deserves all of this love, he was truly brave, not a selfish piece of shit like me...

"Rabbi Yosef died for *his* daughter, for *his* people," Vilém pointed out. "Does that make *him* selfish?"

Of course not!

"Well, you're not selfish for doing what you did to save someone you loved, then!" Vilém proclaimed. "You did it, and you did it for a good reason. That doesn't mean the terrible things you did before are just...erased, but it does mean you're not the same Joseph Klammer who did those things."

But...

"Shut up, you've talked all night, now let me talk!" Vilém exclaimed. "I'm proof that you're a hero. Do you know how many people are here because of what you did? Those four hundred Jews and all of their children and their children's children. Entire generations are going to exist because of you."

I told you before, it's not about the numbers! One murder does not equal one saved life! The seven people I shot? The hundreds I helped deport? What about them? What about their families and descendants that aren't going to exist now?

"They matter too, they matter, Joseph. I'm not telling you to stop feeling guilty about the crimes you actually committed. But...you need to have some perspective. You were a stupid kid. I know that's no excuse, I know other stupid kids like Schwartz never learned, and maybe you just got lucky by meeting Sam. Maybe if you hadn't met him, you would have lived and died a Nazi. But all of those what ifs and comparisons are pointless."

I...

"You're a hero because of *what you did* when push came to shove. You're not just a hero because we respect you, you're a hero because you saw the truth and you did something. There were so many horrible choices you could have made that would have made your life easier, but in the end, you made more good choices than bad. You're a good person. Know how I can tell?"

I'm afraid to ask.

"My great-grandpa liked you and my family is made

up of geniuses," joked Vilém. "But seriously: you went back for Schwartz, you saved him even though you *knew* he'd turn you in. Because you're not arrogant. Because you have empathy. Because you *are* a hero."

Vilém sighed. "And I get it, we kinda turned you into a...non-person, just a flawless hero, and you're not flawless. But nobody is. In those days everyone made mistakes, and back then mistakes destroyed lives. If you want, right after I'm done writing about Raya, I'll write a book about you and include all your dirty laundry. But I'm still gonna call you a hero. You sacrificed your own happiness and comfort, you risked your life and you did the right thing. You are a hero."

You are Sam's descendant.

"I'll take that as a compliment."

You should. I...I really want Doctor Yosef to get the credit he deserves.

"I'll start hunting down documents and testimony," Vilém promised. "He'll get his own exhibit if I have to build it myself."

Ha! All right. But...I'm...scared. I don't know what'll happen if I leave. I don't know what the...standards are. I just...if I were God, I wouldn't let me into Heaven. I just...I don't think I deserve it.

"And that," Vilém said, "is why you're a good person. You're humble, you're good, and you really regret all of the horrible things you did. You're going to Heaven, Joseph Klammer. If you don't get in, nobody gets in."

You're being too nice. I...I'd really like to see Sam again.

"Then go."

I'm just...

"Get outta here, ghost! Go! You've done enough down here! Go on! Go be a homewrecker in Heaven!"

Klammer's spirit laughed. *Fine, Jesus, I'll do whatever you want, just stop nagging me!*

"Do me a favor," Vilém said. "Say hi to my grandpa for me."

I will. I'll give Sam and David a big hug for you. Bye, Vilém. Thanks for listening.

Vilém raised an eyebrow, but forced his mouth to stay shut, not wanting to keep the valiant spirit there for one more minute. He felt a wave of affection wash over him, and suddenly, the ghost was gone.

Vilém stood, stretched, and walked to the front of the exhibit, staring at Joseph Klammer's image. Terribly flawed, terribly brave, terribly human in all the best ways. He smiled and saluted the stalwart Sergeant.

"Bye, hero. Hope you drown in love up there," he said. He fiddled with his flashlight, gazing into Klammer's frozen eyes and cursing his rotten luck. Despite offering him so many answers, Klammer had left him with a question more intense than any little query he had possessed before.

"Who's David?"

AFTERWORD

Thank you for reading Barrack Three!
The sequel, Barrack Two, will be available on December
28, 2020!
If you would like to read more stories like this one,
follow Project 613 on Twitter @Project613Books, on
Facebook, and sign up for updates at Project613Publish-
ing.com!

www.ingramcontent.com/pod-product-compliance
Lightning Source LLC
Chambersburg PA
CBHW020549130626
46552CB00007B/2828